Miffy's
Yummy Cake

Based on the work of **Dick Bruna**
Story written by **Cala Spinner**

SIMON SPOTLIGHT

New York   London   Toronto   Sydney   New Delhi

SIMON SPOTLIGHT

An imprint of Simon & Schuster Children's Publishing Division

1230 Avenue of the Americas, New York, New York 10020

This Simon Spotlight paperback edition January 2017

Published in 2017 by Simon & Schuster, Inc. Publication licensed by Mercis Publishing bv, Amsterdam.

Stories and images are based on the work of Dick Bruna.

'Miffy and Friends' © copyright Mercis Media bv, all rights reserved.

All rights reserved, including the right of reproduction in whole or in part in any form.

SIMON SPOTLIGHT and colophon are registered trademarks of Simon & Schuster, Inc.

For information about special discounts for bulk purchases, please contact Simon & Schuster Special Sales at 1-866-506-1949 or business@simonandschuster.com.

Manufactured in the United States of America 1216 LAK

10 9 8 7 6 5 4 3 2 1

ISBN 978-1-4814-6977-7

ISBN 978-1-4814-6978-4 (eBook)

Today is a special day for Miffy.
She and Daddy are visiting her grandparents!
Grandpa prepares for Miffy's arrival by mowing the lawn.

While Daddy and Grandpa go for a walk, Miffy tells Grandma what she'd like to do today.

"Can we make your pear cake?" Miffy asks. "Please?"

Miffy has heard all about Grandma's delicious pear cake, but she has never eaten it.

"Oh no, Miffy. I'm afraid not," Grandma says. "We haven't got any pears. No pears means no cake . . . unless we go to the market and buy some!"

Miffy cheers.

They will make a cake after all!

The market is a busy place. There are food sellers everywhere.

"Come and get your greens! Lovely sprouts and yummy beans!" calls a seller.

"Big fish! Little fish! Shellfish! Flatfish!" yells the fish seller.

"I have cheese—lovely cheese. Who wants cheese? Just say please!" shouts the cheese seller.

Miffy and Grandma find the fruit seller.

"We want pears," Miffy says.

"Pears?" the fruit seller pauses. "That's bad luck. I've run out. Someone came not long ago and bought all of my pears. Now I don't have any left."

Oh no!

If the fruit seller doesn't have any pears, that means . . .

"No pear cake," Miffy says. She feels disappointed. "And I really wanted to make a pear cake."

"We can make a pear cake next time you visit," Grandma tells Miffy.

The fruit seller returns to calling out his fruit for sale.
"Mango, rhubarb, strawberry!" he shouts.
Strawberry? Miffy perks up. She likes strawberries.
"I know how we can make a cake without pears," Miffy tells Grandma. "We can make a strawberry cake!"

The fruit seller also sells carrots.
Miffy likes carrots, too.
"Let's make a carrot and strawberry cake," Miffy says.
"Why not?" Grandma says. "Let's try something new."

At home Miffy helps Grandma make the cake. She helps measure the ingredients, stirs them together, and pours the batter into a pan. Then Grandma puts it into the oven to bake.

Ding! **The cake is ready.**

"It smells good," Grandma says, taking the cake out of the oven. "I wonder what it will taste like."

When Grandpa and Daddy return, the cake is cool, frosted, and ready to eat.

"Grandma and I have a surprise," Miffy says.

"So do we," Daddy says proudly. "We bought pears so we can make Grandma's pear cake!"

Aha!
"It was you and Grandpa who bought all the pears!"
Miffy says. "We went to the market, but there were no
pears left. So we've made a cake without them."

Grandpa and Daddy are shocked.
"A cake—without pears?" Grandpa asks.
"Yes, it's Miffy's own recipe," Grandma says.
"A carrot and strawberry cake!" Miffy explains.

Miffy serves a slice of cake each to Grandpa and Daddy.
What will they think of Miffy's creation?

Grandpa takes a bite of the cake. Daddy takes a bite of the cake too.

They chew and chew until finally . . .

"Delicious!" Grandpa says. "Even better than Grandma's pear cake!"

"Well done, Miffy," Daddy adds.

Miffy has made a yummy cake indeed!